THE Siege SCARE

SWORD GIRL

THE Siege
SCARE

FRANCES WATTS

ILLUSTRATED BY GREGORY ROGERS

ALLEN&UNWIN
SYDNEY · MELBOURNE · AUCKLAND · LONDON

First published in 2012

Allen & Unwin
83 Alexander Street
Crows Nest NSW 2065
Australia
Phone: (61 2) 8425 0100
Fax: (61 2) 9906 2218
Email: info@allenandunwin.com
Web: www.allenandunwin.com

A Cataloguing-in-Publication entry is available from the National Library
of Australia
www.trove.nla.gov.au

ISBN 978 1 74237 990 6

Cover design by Seymour Designs
Cover illustration by Gregory Rogers
Text design by Seymour Designs
Set in 16/21 pt Adobe Jenson Pro by Seymour Designs
This book was printed in July 2014 by Griffin Press,
168 Cross Keys Road, Salisbury South SA 5106.

10 9 8 7 6 5 4

For Claire, with thanks for the paper

F. W.

For Matt

G. R.

CHAPTER 1

'Goodbye! Good luck!'

Everyone at Flamant Castle had poured out of the castle gate to see off the knights.

Tommy waved until her arm hurt, then leaned against the railing of the bridge and watched till the knights were out of sight. Sir Walter the Bald, the nobleman who owned Flamant Castle, rode at the head of the procession. Sir Benedict, the

castle's bravest knight, was at his right hand. They were on their way east to Roses Castle. A month ago, Sir Percy and the knights of Roses had come to Flamant for a tournament. Now Sir Percy was holding a tournament at his castle, and nearly all the knights and squires of Flamant would be competing.

'I bet Sir Hugh is disappointed about being left behind,' Tommy said as the knight escorted Sir Walter's wife, Lady Beatrix the Bored, back inside the castle walls.

'Someone has to guard Flamant Castle and its lands,' Lil pointed out. 'But you're right. Nothing much will happen around here until the knights return – which suits me just fine.' The black and white cat

stretched and yawned. 'There's been too much activity for my taste. I'm looking forward to a bit of peace and quiet and a warm patch of sun in the great courtyard.'

She began to pad across the bridge towards the castle gate and Tommy fell into step beside her.

'What about you, Tommy? The armoury will seem very quiet after all the hustle and bustle of getting the knights' swords ready for the tournament.'

'What I'd really like to do is spend some time looking after the Old Wrecks,' Tommy confided. 'I've been so busy with the other swords I feel like I've neglected them.'

'I'm sure they wouldn't agree,' said Lil. The Old Wrecks *had* been neglected for a long time, sitting dusty and unused in

the darkest corner of the sword chamber. But when Tommy had become Keeper of the Blades she'd polished and sharpened them and found, to her astonishment, that the swords were inhabited by the spirits of their last owners.

For once the armoury was silent when Tommy entered. Smith had gone into town to see the blacksmith about some new shields, and there was no sign of lazy Reynard, the Keeper of the Bows.

Tommy went through the doorway to the left of the forge and into the sword chamber.

'Sir Walter and the knights have left for Roses,' she announced to the Old Wrecks.

'What a pity you couldn't go with them, dearie,' said a sabre from the rack in the corner.

Tommy, who had fought in the tournament at Flamant when one of the squires was injured, shrugged. 'I'm of more use here, Nursie,' she said as she pulled the sabre from the rack. 'After all, Sir Hugh and his men will still need their swords cared for.'

'Our sword girl has an admirable devotion to duty,' said the dignified voice of Bevan Brumm, a long-handled dagger.

'She does,' said the slender, slightly curved sword that was Jasper Swann. Jasper had been a squire, and was close to Tommy's own age when he'd fallen ill and died. 'But tell us again about how you won your jousting bout at the tournament, Sword Girl.'

So Tommy settled down with her file

and whetstone for sharpening, and a pot of clove-scented oil for polishing, and described her victory.

'Ooh, well done, Sword Girl,' said Nursie appreciatively. 'Of course, my little darling won every bout he entered …'

Tommy thought she heard a groan from Bevan Brumm.

Nursie loved telling stories about her 'little darling', which was what she had called Sir Walter the Bald when he was a boy and she was his nursemaid.

'He had so much energy, you see,' she recalled fondly. 'He was always up to something. Oh, the mischief! One time he went missing for a whole day. My stars, I was in such a panic. I finally found him in the cellar. He said he'd been playing in

an old tunnel. He told me it ran under the castle walls and underneath the town and came out in Skellibones Forest. Playing in dark, dirty tunnels was not at all what a young nobleman should be doing, I told him.'

'There's a tunnel running from here to the forest?' asked Tommy, interested.

'Oh no,' said Nursie. 'I'm sure he was just making up tales to fool his old Nursie.'

'There used to be rumours about a tunnel when I was a squire,' Jasper said. 'But no one ever seemed to know where it was.'

'I often wished for a tunnel when I was riding through the forest on dark, moonless nights,' Bevan Brumm said. He had been a merchant when he was alive, and had travelled widely. 'There's nothing worse than expecting a bandit to leap out from behind every tree.'

Tommy gulped. 'I hope *I* never have to travel through a forest on a dark, moonless night,' she said.

'If you ever do, you can take me with you, Sword Girl,' Jasper offered.

'Thanks, Jasper, I will,' said Tommy as a voice called, 'Hello? Is anyone here?'

Tommy ran to the door to see Sir Hugh pacing around the armoury.

'Hello, Sir Hugh. There's just me here, sir – Smith is in town. Can I help you?'

The knight held out his sword. 'Indeed you can, Tommy. I need my sword sharpened, and there'll be twenty more to be readied, too.'

'Twenty swords?' Tommy said in surprise.

Just when she'd thought things would be quiet in the sword chamber!

'That's right, and as fast as you can.' Sir Hugh's expression was grim. 'Yesterday Sir Benedict sent a couple of men out to patrol our western border and they've just returned with bad news. They spied a raiding party of a dozen of Sir Malcolm the Mean's knights from Malice Castle riding in our direction.'

Tommy put a hand to her mouth. 'Sir

Malcolm's knights are coming here?' she whispered.

'Sir Malcolm must have heard that Flamant's knights are away at the tournament at Roses,' Sir Hugh said. 'He obviously didn't reckon on the fact that some of us would be staying behind. But Sir Walter and Sir Benedict are smarter than that. I'm taking twenty men out to confront the raiding party. How soon can you have our swords ready?'

Within half an hour the armoury was as busy as it had ever been. Smith had returned from town to find Tommy hard at work. When she had explained why she suddenly had twenty swords to sharpen, the smith had immediately picked up a file and begun to help her. They worked side by side until finally, just as the sun was sinking beneath the battlements, they were ready.

Tommy could hear the stamping of hooves on the flagstones outside as Sir Hugh and his knights brought their horses round then hastened into the armoury to collect their swords.

After the last man had mounted his horse, Tommy and Smith followed them through the castle gate and onto the bridge. This time Tommy didn't wave cheerfully as she watched the small band of knights gallop towards the setting sun.

'Do you think they'll be able to fight off Sir Malcolm's raiding party, Smith?' she asked.

Smith let out a heavy sigh. 'Let's hope so, Sword Girl,' he said. 'Because if they don't, we've no one left to protect us.'

CHAPTER 2

TOMMY SLEPT RESTLESSLY that night, and when she sat at the long kitchen table for her breakfast the next morning, she could only manage a couple of bites of bread.

'What's got into you this morning, Thomasina?' the cook wanted to know.

'I'm sorry, Mrs Moon,' said Tommy as she pushed her plate away. 'I'm just worried about the raiding party from Malice Castle. What if Sir Hugh can't stop them?'

The cook snorted. 'Sir Malcolm the Mean's knights are no match for the men of Flamant Castle,' she declared. 'You stop your moping about, girl. Sir Hugh will be back with good news before the sun is high, you mark my words.'

Tommy went to work in the sword chamber, determined to sharpen every bladed weapon in the armoury. Mrs Moon had told her not to worry, but Smith's long face told a different story. Even Lil, who had been so eager to bask in the sun on the flagstones of the courtyard, was unsettled.

Midday came, and though the sun had reached its highest point, there was no word

from Sir Hugh. As the sun sank behind the battlements once more, still nothing had been heard.

That night Tommy had bad dreams about fire and people shouting. She woke with a start to realise that she *had* heard something. She pulled on her tunic and leggings and ran outside to the great courtyard.

Instead of a dark, star-speckled sky, the night was lit up with flames! Just like in her dream, people were running and yelling, as flaming arrows the size of broomsticks hurtled over the castle walls.

The wooden roof above a walkway between two towers was on fire, and Tommy watched in horror as an arrow landed on the roof of the well only metres away from her. It burst into flames and Tommy shrank back against the wall.

Suddenly Mrs Moon appeared, her long nightgown flapping around her ankles.

'Come back inside, Thomasina,' she ordered. 'It's not safe, child.'

She grasped Tommy's arm and tried to usher her into the safety of the

kitchen but Tommy pulled away and ran across the courtyard. She had to find Lil!

There was a rush of air as an enormous boulder hit the ground in front of her with a *thud*, cracking several flagstones. Tommy's heart started to race – the boulder had only just missed her! Whoever was outside the walls must have a giant catapult to be able to hurl such huge rocks.

'Lil!' she shouted. 'Lil, where are you?' The courtyard was so full of people running about in a panic, she could barely see or hear anything.

She reached Lil's favourite sleeping spot in the corner of the courtyard, gasping as another flaming arrow landed near her.

In an instant Smith was beside her, beating at the flames with a sack.

'What's happening?' Tommy cried.

'A siege!' he roared above the noise. 'A hundred or more knights from Malice Castle. The raiding party to the west was just a decoy. While Sir Hugh is off chasing them, the rest of Sir Malcolm's knights have circled around and approached from the north.'

The ground beneath their feet quaked as another boulder landed nearby, and Tommy's heart quaked too.

Flamant Castle was under attack!

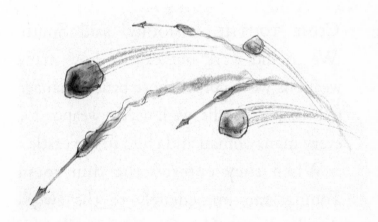

CHAPTER 3

'COME TO THE ARMOURY,' said Smith. 'We should work out exactly how many weapons we've got. If those brutes manage to breach the walls, we'll need a weapon for every man, woman and child in the castle.'

When they entered the dim room Tommy ran immediately to the sword chamber to see if her friends were all right. To her relief, the black and white cat was

crouched in the
corner beside
the Old Wrecks.

'Lil! Thank
goodness
you're safe!'

'Only just,'
replied Lil.
'I was almost
hit by an arrow.'
The cat, who always
seemed so calm, looked shaken.

'What is it, Sword Girl? What's going
on?' Jasper asked urgently.

'It's the knights of Malice Castle,' Tommy
said. 'We're under siege!'

Back in the armoury, Smith was stoking
the fire.

'We're in a tight spot here, Sword Girl,' he said. 'Sir Malcolm's men have the castle and the town surrounded. We'll hold them off for as long as we can, but even if Sir Hugh and his men returned now, I don't like their chances against a hundred enemies. We need Sir Benedict and the rest of the knights, but whether we'll be able to defend the castle until they return is anyone's guess.'

'Can't we get a message to Sir Benedict?' Tommy asked. 'Then he'd return straight away.'

The smith shook his head. 'If only it were that simple. But Roses Castle is a full day's ride away. And we can't risk opening the gate to let a horse and rider out. The invaders would storm the castle.' He stared gloomily into the fire. 'I'm afraid we're trapped here until help comes. *If help comes …*'

Tommy shivered. So the castle walls that protected them were also their prison. 'But they won't be able to get in, will they?'

'They'll be having a good go,' said Smith. 'They'll try to crash through the gate with a battering ram long enough to reach across the moat, and they'll try to scale the walls with long ladders.' He poked at the fire. 'We'll have to make sure the guards in the towers have poles so they can knock the attackers off their ladders.'

'I wish I still had my lance from the tournament,' Tommy declared. 'I'd knock them off.'

'You're right, Sword Girl – lances would do the job nicely. But all our lances are with the squires who'll be jousting at Roses. Unless…' He looked up from the fire. 'There might be some old weapons in the cellar.'

'I thought the cellar was for storing food?' said Tommy.

'Did you ever go down to the cellar when you worked in the kitchen, Sword Girl?' asked the smith.

'No,' said Tommy. The door to the cellar was locked with a key, and the cook never let anyone go down there. 'Mrs Moon always said that the cellar was her treasure vault and she wasn't letting anyone near her treasure.'

The smith nodded. 'True enough. If we're to survive under siege, the castle's food stores will be more valuable to us than all Sir Walter's gold and Lady Beatrix's jewels. But the cellar is vast – there's more than food down there. The castle's old weapons will be there too. I want you to go down to the cellar and see what weapons we have, then report back to me.'

'Yes, Smith,' said Tommy.

'Oh, and Sword Girl? You might want to take a weapon with you – just in case.'

Tommy darted back into the sword chamber. 'Jasper,' she said to the slender sword, 'will you come with me to the cellar? Smith wants me to look for weapons down there.'

'Of course,' said Jasper, and Tommy took hold of the narrow wooden grip and slid the sword from the rack.

'You're going to the cellar?' quavered Nursie. 'Oh, please be careful, my dears. What if my little darling really did find a tunnel in the cellar? The invaders might find it too!'

Tommy stared at the sabre. 'Nursie, you're brilliant!' she exclaimed.

'I – I am?' said Nursie.

'Yes,' said Tommy. 'Smith said we couldn't get a message to Sir Benedict because there was no way out of the castle. But maybe there *is* a way.'

'Good thinking, Tommy,' said Lil.

'Maybe you could come too, Lil, and help me look,' Tommy suggested. 'You're much better at seeing in the dark than I am.'

'An excellent plan,' said Bevan Brumm.

'What's an excellent plan?' Nursie asked.

'Why am I brilliant? I don't understand.'
She sounded bewildered.

Tommy lifted her sword. 'The tunnel,'
she said. 'Never mind about the invaders –
I'm going to find it first!'

CHAPTER 4

THE PALE LIGHT of dawn was creeping across the sky when Tommy stepped into the courtyard. The shower of flaming arrows had slowed, leaving charred patches of stone.

She picked her way across the courtyard towards the kitchen, skirting boulders and taking care to avoid the smouldering piles of ashes as the last of the arrows burned down.

'Please!' a voice nearby said, and Tommy turned to see the small, round figure of the physician. He appeared to be pleading with the pigeon, who was perched on a low wall.

'Certainly not,' the bird was saying in a cross voice. 'Your constant demand for my droppings is an insult to my skill and training.'

'But a guard in one of the watchtowers

has suffered a nasty burn,' the physician argued. 'I need to mix your droppings with some grated cucumber to make a cure.'

The pigeon groaned. 'Very well. If you must.'

Tommy hurried on, knowing how the pigeon disliked people watching when he gave his droppings.

She entered the kitchen to find Mrs Moon standing by the enormous fireplace, stirring a large pot of soup.

The cook's face was creased with worry as she stared at the simmering soup. 'He's a devil is Sir Malcolm the Mean,' she was muttering to herself. 'If Sir Benedict doesn't return in time to save us, we might find ourselves in the dungeons of Malice Castle. Or worse ...'

Tommy's heart thudded. She didn't want to know what could be worse than the dungeons!

'Mrs Moon,' she said, 'Smith asked me to go down to the cellar to look for old weapons.'

'Thomasina!' The cook put a hand to her chest. 'You startled me.' She shook her wooden spoon at Tommy. 'This isn't a good time to go sneaking up on people, girl.'

'Sorry, Mrs Moon,' Tommy murmured, though she hadn't meant to sneak up.

'What's that you're wanting? The cellar? That's a fine idea. I don't know how long this siege might last. I'd better go down myself to check the stores.'

The cook led the way to a small wooden door in the scullery and pulled a big iron key from her pocket. She took a candlestick from a niche in the wall and gestured for Tommy to take one too.

'It'll be mighty dark down there,' she warned.

Down, down, down they went, into the dark. The cold of the stone steps seeped through Tommy's clothes and shoes to chill her bones.

She clutched Jasper Swann in one hand and the candlestick in the other. 'Are you there, Lil?' she whispered. There was no answer, but Tommy felt something warm brush against her leg and knew her friend was beside her.

Finally the stairs stopped, and Tommy lifted her candle. They were standing in a small, low-ceilinged room that had a doorway leading off to the left and another leading off to the right.

'The food stores are kept in these rooms under the kitchen,' Mrs Moon told her, pointing to the doorway on the left. 'But the cellar runs all the way under the great hall as well. That's where the weapons are likely to be.' She gestured to the right with her candle.

Tommy set off, entering a room that had barrels of ale and cider stacked against the walls. A door led to another room full of barrels and then another. As she walked through room after room her heart sank. She found dusty piles of tapestries that must have once hung on the walls of the great hall, a room full of bolts of cloth that had been long forgotten (except by the insects that had chewed holes in it), and another room full of tarnished armour. Her spirits rose slightly when she found a room of rusty shields and blunt swords. They weren't in very good condition but they would be better than nothing. There were no lances, though, and to her dismay there was no sign of a tunnel.

'Perhaps Nursie was right the first time,' she said aloud. 'Maybe there was no tunnel, and Sir Walter was just making it up.'

'And yet it makes so much sense to have a tunnel,' Jasper pointed out. 'There has to be some secret way out of the castle during a siege.'

'I agree,' said Lil, her eyes glinting in the dark.

'I suppose if it's secret, it has to be well hidden,' Tommy said. 'Let's look again.'

They went back through the series of rooms, this time poking into every dark corner, but there was still no sign of a tunnel. They had almost reached the stairs to the kitchen when Tommy heard Lil's muffled voice.

'I think I've found something.'

'Where are you?' said Tommy, raising her candle so that light bounced off the barrels stacked against the walls.

'Here.'

Tommy lowered the candle to see the black and white cat emerging from a tiny space behind a barrel. She set the candle on the ground and lay Jasper beside it, then tugged at the barrel.

'It's too heavy,' she said. 'I can't lift it.'

'Come on, Tommy,' Jasper urged. 'Don't try to lift it – just drag it.'

The muscles in Tommy's arms strained as she heaved until the barrel began to move slowly across the floor. When she had slid

it far enough she dropped to her knees and wriggled behind the barrel. Lil was right: there was an opening – but it was barely tall enough for Tommy to enter on her hands and knees, and the sides were so narrow she couldn't even stretch her arms out.

'It's very small,' she said doubtfully.

But when she held up the candle she felt a twinge of excitement at what she saw. 'It goes for a long way,' she said, 'and the walls are very well made.' She ran her hands along the stone sides. 'This must be it!'

'Thomasina!' Mrs Moon's voice echoed through the stone rooms. 'Thomasina, where are you?'

'Coming, Mrs Moon.'

Tommy scrambled out of the tunnel and pushed the barrel back into place.

'What have you been up to, girl?' the cook scolded, smoothing down Tommy's mop of hair with an impatient swipe of her hand. 'You look like you've been dragged through a hedge backwards. Did you find what you were looking for?'

'Yes, Mrs Moon,' said Tommy. 'I did.'

CHAPTER 5

TOMMY RUSHED BACK to the armoury and told Smith that although there'd been no lances, she had found a room full of old swords and shields.

'Never mind about the lances,' Smith said. 'We can knock their ladders over with brooms if we have to.'

But when she described the condition of the swords and shields, he grunted. 'We don't have time to bring them up to scratch. We'll just have to work with what we've got. I want you to sharpen every bladed weapon in the sword chamber,' he instructed.

'I'm almost done,' Tommy told him. 'I made a good start on that yesterday.'

Smith raised his eyebrows. 'You did, eh? Good thinking, Sword Girl.' He called out, 'Did you hear that, Reynard? Our sword girl started sharpening all the blades yesterday.'

There was a snarl from the bow chamber, but no answer. Tommy winced. Reynard already hated her because she'd been made Keeper of the Blades instead of him; he'd probably hate her even more now.

When she stepped into the sword chamber with Lil and Jasper she was met with the anxious voices of Nursie and Bevan Brumm.

'Oh, thank goodness you're back,' said Nursie. 'We were fearing the worst, weren't we, Bevan Brumm?'

'Indeed, we had begun to hold grave fears for your safety,' the dagger admitted.

'I'm sorry you were worried,' said Tommy. 'But guess what? We found the tunnel!'

'You did?' exclaimed Nursie. 'Then my little darling was telling the truth all along.'

'So you can send a horse and rider through the tunnel to carry a message to Sir Benedict, and save Flamant Castle,' said Bevan Brumm. 'Well done, Sword Girl!'

Tommy dropped onto her stool. 'I'm afraid we can't do that,' she said, her spirits sinking again. 'The tunnel's not big enough for a horse and rider. It's barely big enough for me.'

Silence fell in the sword chamber. Tommy prepared her file and whetstone and set about sharpening and polishing the swords she hadn't finished the day before.

Hours had passed by the time she took the last sword – a short thrusting sword – from the long rack. There must be a way to send for help, she thought as she began to sharpen the blade. But they couldn't get a horse and rider through the tunnel under the walls, and a messenger couldn't very well climb over the walls, not without the invaders seeing. Oh, if only she could fly, then she'd be able to get a message to Sir Benedict ...

Tommy raised her head as a thought

struck her. The pigeon could fly! She remembered the cross voice saying, *Your constant demand for droppings is an insult to my skills and training.* Of course! He was a carrier pigeon, trained to carry messages!

Tommy stood up. 'Lil,' she said, 'the pigeon could do it! He could fly to Roses Castle with a message.'

Lil, who had been grooming her whiskers, paused. 'You're right,' she said, her eyes brightening.

'I'm going to find him,' said Tommy, and she hurried out to the great courtyard.

She was pleased to find the pigeon slumped on the low wall where she had seen him earlier. He looked exhausted.

'Pigeon, I'm so glad you're here,' said Tommy. 'I need your help.'

The pigeon raised a limp wing. 'Sorry, but I haven't got a single dropping left in me.'

'I don't need your droppings,' said Tommy. 'I'd like you to carry a message.'

The pigeon straightened. 'A message? Well, why didn't you say so? Carrying messages is what I do best.'

Tommy clapped her hands together. 'Hooray! Then you can go to Sir Benedict at Roses Castle.'

The pigeon slumped again. 'I don't think I can, Sword Girl. I've given so many droppings that it's left me weak. If it were somewhere closer, perhaps I could manage it, but Roses is so far. I'd never make it ...'

Tommy tried to hide her disappointment. 'That's all right. Thanks anyway.'

She returned to the sword chamber and sat down with a sigh. The pigeon was right – it was a long way to Roses. Even if she squeezed through the tunnel herself, it would take her days to get there on foot, and she might arrive too late. If she had a horse, she'd ride to Roses. Though she could never get a horse through the tunnel, she reminded herself.

She dipped a rag into her pot of clove-scented oil and began to polish the blade of the thrusting sword.

But what if she could find a horse outside the castle? Then she could sneak through the tunnel, get the horse and ride to Roses. Where could she find a horse, though?

'Bevan Brumm,' she said, 'when you were a merchant and you needed to hire a horse, where did you go?'

'I would usually enquire at an inn,' the dagger replied. 'The innkeeper at The Twisted Tree, a mile or so into Skellibones Forest, kept horses for hire.'

'Skellibones Forest?' said Tommy. 'That's perfect!'

'What are you thinking, Sword Girl?' asked Jasper.

'We can't get a horse and rider through the tunnel, but I could go through the tunnel myself and then hire a horse at The Twisted Tree,' Tommy explained.

'It would be quicker if you could get a message to the innkeeper so that he could have a horse ready and waiting,' Lil suggested.

'But how could I get a message to—' Tommy stopped. 'The pigeon! He said he couldn't make it all the way to Roses, but he could take a message to somewhere closer. He could carry a message to the innkeeper.'

The cat nodded. 'The question is,' she said, 'who should write the message? It should be someone the innkeeper knows and would obey without question.'

Tommy thought for a minute, then smiled. 'I know just the person,' she said.

Tommy brushed at her tunic and tugged it straight, then ran across the great hall and climbed the steps to the upper floor of the south tower.

She drew in a breath as she gazed around the bower that was Lady Beatrix the Bored's private room. Colourful tapestries hung on the walls and the big bed in the centre of the room was scattered with beautifully embroidered cushions and covers. Lady Beatrix herself was lying on the bed with her lady-in-waiting sitting on a bench beside her.

'Sieges are terrible, Eliza,' Lady Beatrix was saying. 'And terribly boring, too. What will happen if Sir Walter and Sir Benedict don't return in time to save us?'

'I couldn't say, my lady,' said Eliza.

'Excuse me, my lady,' Tommy said from the doorway.

Lady Beatrix sat up. 'Eliza, look – it's the little sword girl from the armoury. The one who was my champion at the tournament last month. What are you doing here, Sword Girl?'

'My lady, I have a plan to save the castle – but I need your help.'

'A plan to save the castle? My dear girl, I admire your spirit, but how can a little thing like you save the castle?'

'I've found a tunnel that goes under the castle walls and comes out in Skellibones Forest. If I can arrange to have a horse waiting for me, I could ride to Roses to fetch Sir Walter and the knights. Would you write a message to the innkeeper of The Twisted Tree for me, my lady, asking him to ready a horse? I'll get the pigeon to carry the message to him.'

Lady Beatrix was staring at Tommy with

her mouth open. 'Why, Sword Girl,' she said, 'I beg your pardon for doubting you. I most certainly will write a message for you.' She turned to her lady-in-waiting. 'Eliza, fetch me some ink and paper.'

When Eliza returned, Lady Beatrix immediately began to write. When she was done she blotted the paper, folded it and fixed it with her wax seal.

'There,' she said, as she handed the message to Tommy. 'I've outlined your plan and instructed the innkeeper to prepare a horse for the Keeper of the Blades and have it ready just before dawn, when it's darkest.'

'Thank you, my lady,' Tommy said, turning for the door.

'Sword Girl?'

Tommy stopped. 'Yes, my lady?'

'We don't want you to catch a chill on your journey. Eliza, fetch one of my woollen cloaks – the dark blue one – and one of Sir Walter's belts. She'll need it to hold her sword while she rides. Oh, and one of my ribbons, too, Eliza; you shall be my champion again, Sword Girl.'

As Tommy hurried down the stairs, the cloak around her shoulders and the belt around her waist, she heard Lady Beatrix say, 'Do you know what I like about that girl, Eliza? She never bores me.'

CHAPTER 6

THE SUN WAS LOW in the sky when Tommy stepped from the great hall into the courtyard.

'Pigeon,' she called. 'Where are you?'

'Here!' a voice croaked.

Tommy traced the sound to a bedraggled pile of feathers sitting on the edge of a water trough. If anything, he looked worse than when she had seen him earlier.

'Pigeon, are you okay?' she asked.

The bird waved a weary wing. 'I had to give more droppings,' he gasped out.

'Oh no,' Tommy said. 'I was hoping you'd carry an important message for me. Not to Roses – just to The Twisted Tree in Skellibones Forest. It might be our only chance to save Flamant!'

With some effort, the pigeon got to his feet and stuck out a leg. 'If it will save the castle, I have to do it,' he said.

Tommy tied the message to the pigeon's leg using the ribbon Lady Beatrix had

given her. She hoped the lady wouldn't mind.

'Don't let any of the knights of Malice see you,' she warned.

The pigeon was already flexing his wings, ready to depart.

'Don't worry,' he said. 'This is what I was trained for.'

Tommy watched as the pigeon rose into the sky and soared out of sight. Then she headed for the kitchen. There was one more part of the plan she had to put into place.

The kitchen was bustling with preparations for supper. A dozen kitchen girls were arranged around the long table, peeling potatoes, slicing carrots and dicing turnips. The cook was barking out

instructions, but she broke off when she caught sight of Tommy in the doorway.

'What is it now, Thomasina? I don't have time for … what on earth are you wearing, girl?'

'It's a cloak,' said Tommy.

'I can see it's a cloak, girl,' the cook snapped. 'But it's not *your* cloak, is it? What I want to know is why *you* are wearing it.'

'Lady Beatrix lent it to me.'

Mrs Moon's eyes went wide. 'Lady Beatrix? If you're lying to me, Thomasina, I'll twist your ear so hard it'll come right off in my hand, so I will.'

'Mrs Moon, I need to speak to you,' said Tommy. 'In private.'

The cook's face grew serious. 'Very well,' she said.

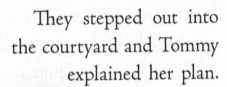

They stepped out into
the courtyard and Tommy
explained her plan.
'So I need the
key to the cellar,'
she finished.

Without a word,
Mrs Moon
reached into
her pocket,
pulled out the big iron key and gave it
to Tommy. Then she put her hand on
Tommy's shoulder. 'You'll be needing a
good supper, too,' she said. 'Come and I'll
give you a bowl of soup.'

It was dark when Tommy returned to the armoury. There was no sign of Smith or Reynard, but she found Lil waiting in the sword chamber.

'I saw the pigeon in the courtyard a few minutes ago,' the cat said.

Tommy's heart almost stopped beating as she waited to hear what Lil said next.

'The message was received and understood.'

Phew! Tommy sat down on the floor and leaned against the wall. 'Then all I have to do now is wait till the dead of night,' she said.

Tommy was dozing against the wall of the sword chamber when she was woken by the touch of a paw against her cheek.

'Tommy?' It was Lil. 'It's time.'

Tommy stood up and stretched. 'Ready, Jasper?' she asked as she closed her hand around the sword's narrow grip.

'I'm ready,' came the reply.

The sky was glowing from the fires of the invaders outside the walls, but inside the walls the great courtyard was deserted. Not everyone was asleep, though. The men of the castle lined the battlements, prepared to repel any invasion.

With Lil by her side, Tommy walked through the dark kitchen to the scullery, and unlocked the small wooden door.

Down into the cold cellar she went, carrying a candle in one hand, her sword in the other. Her heart was pounding now at the thought of what she was about to do.

In the third room under the great hall, she set her candle and sword down and pulled back the barrel that hid the opening of the tunnel.

'Here I go,' she said, picking up Jasper once more and slipping him beneath the belt around her waist. 'I'll need both hands to crawl through the tunnel.' She swallowed. 'So I'll have to leave the candle behind.'

'Travel safely, Tommy,' Lil said as Tommy dropped to her knees and squeezed behind the barrel and into the tunnel. And then Tommy was alone – alone in the deepest, darkest, coldest place she had ever been …

CHAPTER 7

TOMMY CRAWLED ALONG the chill damp stones, feeling her way with her hands. The weight of the stone above her head seemed to press down on her in the small passage, so narrow there wasn't even room to turn around if she should meet an enemy coming towards her in the dark. She began to breathe more quickly, and then a new fear struck her: she was deep underground and there was nowhere for fresh air to enter the tunnel!

On and on she went, fighting off the frightening thoughts that threatened to overwhelm her. Surely she must be nearing the end of the tunnel?

'It's taking too long,' she said. 'What if we were wrong? What if the tunnel doesn't actually go anywhere?'

Then a dim glow pierced the darkness and something brushed against her face.

'What is it?' Jasper asked as Tommy, stifling a scream, drew back in alarm.

'I don't know,' Tommy whispered. She put out a hand to feel. 'It's leaves,' she said excitedly. 'Jasper, we've made it!'

'Careful now,' said Jasper. 'We don't know what's waiting for us out there.'

Tommy pulled the sword from her belt and held it out as she cautiously parted the leaves. She was dreading a shout, a cry of discovery. What if the knights of Malice were in the forest, too? But all was silent.

A road stretched ahead of her, the trees casting eerie shadows in the moonlight. Tommy had just stepped out of the shelter of the trees when a cloud floated across the moon. She began to tremble. It was a dark, moonless night, like the ones Bevan Brumm had described. What if there were bandits? She reached down to touch Jasper's grip. She had a sword, she reminded herself, and she knew how to use it. But all the same ...

Her heart hammered in her chest as she began to run, stumbling in the dark but

never slowing, till at last she saw something glowing through the trees.

It was the inn, and there was a single lantern burning in the window.

With a cry of relief she entered the yard.

'Sword Girl?'

Tommy jumped, her hand flying to the sword in her belt as a quiet voice spoke in her ear.

It was the innkeeper, and he was holding a bridle. 'This is my own horse, Ned,' he said, and Tommy stroked the neck of a stocky horse.

'Hello, Ned,' she said. 'Thank you – thank you both – for helping.'

'I hope your plan works, Sword Girl,' the innkeeper said. 'Or I'm afraid Flamant is doomed.'

CHAPTER 8

THE CLOUDS PARTED and the moon lit her way as Tommy rode through the night. She and Ned took the forest at a gallop, then followed the road east through fields and meadows, and along a winding river.

The sun rose over the tops of the trees that lined the river and kept rising and rising until it was directly overhead. On she rode, and by the time she had her first glimpse of Roses Castle, squatting huge and grey in the middle of a plain shimmering with grasses, the sun was beginning to sink once more.

As she drew nearer she could see the tents and viewing platforms of the tournament, but there were no knights or squires on the jousting field. The day's competition would be over and they'd be gathering in the great hall for the evening's feast.

Tommy rode up to the castle gate, breathing hard from her long ride.

A guard stepped forward to bar her way. 'Who goes there?'

'I'm the Keeper of the Blades from Flamant Castle,' Tommy panted. 'I need to speak to Sir Benedict urgently.'

The guard looked her up and down.

'All right,' he said. 'You may pass. I'll have someone fetch Sir Benedict.'

Tommy rode Ned into the great courtyard of Roses Castle. When she slid from his back she found her legs were so weak they could barely hold her. She was leaning against the stocky brown horse for support when Sir Benedict entered the courtyard at a run, Sir Walter and Sir Percy close behind.

'Tommy, what is it?' Sir Benedict demanded. 'Has something happened at Flamant?'

'We're under siege!' Tommy said. 'Sir Malcolm the Mean sent a raiding party to the western border as a decoy, and when Sir Hugh rode out to meet them with our remaining knights, the knights from

Malice attacked. They've got Flamant Castle and the town surrounded!' Quickly she outlined the plan she had come up with to escape from the castle and ride for help.

Sir Walter's face lit up when Tommy told how Lady Beatrix had written the message to the innkeeper and how the pigeon, worn out though he was, had delivered it.

'I trained that my pigeon myself,' he said proudly. Then he peered at Tommy. 'Why, that's my wife's best cloak,' he said, pointing to the cloak Tommy wore. 'And *my* best belt!'

'Lady Beatrix was kind enough to lend them to me,' said Tommy.

'My poor, dear Beatrix,' said Sir Walter, his eyes clouding over. 'How terrified she

must be. Sir Benedict, we must leave at once to fight off the invaders!'

'We'll join you,' Sir Percy declared. 'We must teach Sir Malcolm a lesson.'

'Tommy, you've had a long ride. Would you like to stay here and rest, or will you ride with us?' Sir Benedict asked.

'I'll ride with you, sir,' said Tommy, standing tall despite her tiredness.

In next to no time, the knights of Flamant and Roses had assembled in the great courtyard of Roses Castle.

'Ride out!' Sir Percy called, and soon the courtyard rang with the sound of thundering hooves.

For all the long journey through the

night, Tommy rode alongside her hero, Sir Benedict. The rhythm of their horses' hooves beat out the passing seconds, minutes and hours. Would they make it in time? Tommy thought of her friends, trapped behind the castle walls, and wished they could go faster. But the horses were already galloping at full stretch.

It was early morning as Flamant Castle came into view.

'Look!' Tommy cried, pointing.

The invaders from Malice had set up dozens of long ladders and were swarming up the castle walls. The guards of Flamant Castle were on the verge of being overrun.

Sir Walter, Sir Benedict and Sir Percy drew together for a quick

discussion then, at a nod from the two noblemen, Flamant Castle's bravest knight began to call out instructions.

'Sir Alistair, go after the enemies surrounding the town!'

'Yes, Sir Benedict!' Sir Alistair and a group of men from Roses Castle galloped towards the town walls to chase away the knights who had Flamant surrounded.

'Archers, ride ahead!' Sir Benedict ordered, and the archers galloped off, firing arrows at the invaders on the ladders.

Almost instantly, the men who had been swarming up the castle walls began to swarm down, ducking and dodging the arrows raining over them. Meanwhile, those on the ground, seeing hundreds of Flamant Castle's finest knights riding towards them with swords aloft, ran for their horses.

The guards in the castle towers began to cheer as the invaders fled. 'Hooray! We're saved!'

The drawbridge was lowered and those who had been trapped inside the castle crowded through the gate to cheer home their rescuers. Tommy was still too far away to make out their faces, but she began to wave anyway, hoping that Lil might see her – or perhaps Lil had gone down to the moat to check on the crocodiddle? Tommy's heart gave a lurch as she realised how frightening the siege must have been for the poor crocodiddle, trapped outside the walls with all the noise and commotion.

She scanned the banks of the moat

anxiously, hoping for a glimpse of him. When she saw a movement in the bushes, she gave a sigh of relief – her friend must be emerging from his hiding place. Then she gasped; instead of a scaly green reptile, a figure dressed in a black tunic was slipping from the cover of the bushes. It was one of Sir Malcolm's knights!

Tommy watched, expecting him to flee after his companions, but instead he was creeping in the other direction. With a start, Tommy realised he was heading towards the catapult, which was already loaded with a huge boulder – aimed right at the drawbridge where all the castle's inhabitants had gathered. She had to stop him!

Tommy tightened the reins and leaned

forward in the saddle, urging Ned into a gallop.

The enemy knight must have heard Ned's hooves pounding across the field because he glanced up and, seeing Tommy and the horse streaking towards the catapult, broke into a run.

'Faster, Ned!' Tommy said, bending low over the horse's neck.

The ground passed beneath her in a blur and Tommy's pulse raced in time with the horse's steps. They had to reach the catapult first – they had to!

'Whoa!' Tommy pulled on the reins as they reached the wooden structure and slid from the horse's back a split second before the enemy knight ran up.

'Out of my way, girl!' he barked.

'No!' Tommy said, though she trembled with fear as she gazed at the black-clad man towering over her.

'I said *move!*'

The knight took a step towards her and Tommy pulled Jasper Swann from her belt.

'Don't take another step,' she told him, brandishing the sword.

'I warned you, girl,' the knight hissed as he pulled his own sword from his belt.

Without thinking, Tommy stepped forward and, with a powerful downward stroke, knocked the knight's sword from his grasp.

'Wh-what?' he stammered, looking at his empty hand in disbelief.

'You don't want to get in a fight with our sword girl,' said a voice behind Tommy.

She spun around to see Sir Benedict, still on horseback. She'd been so intent on the enemy, she hadn't even heard him ride up.

'Well done, Tommy,' Sir Benedict said. 'You took care of him.'

The knight from Malice was now running away across the field, with two of Flamant's knights riding after him.

Sir Benedict gave her a nod. 'Now let's go home.'

Tommy grasped Ned's reins and put her foot in the stirrup, then swung onto the horse's back.

Together she and Sir Benedict cantered back to Sir Walter, Sir Percy and the procession of knights riding towards the castle.

'Sir Thomas,' Sir Walter was shouting as they rejoined the others, 'take fifty men and continue west to find Sir Hugh.'

With a burst of speed, fifty horses peeled off from the main group and followed Sir Thomas west after the fleeing knights of Malice.

'Sword Girl, take the front!'

Tommy's head jerked up. Had she heard Sir Walter correctly?

Sir Benedict was grinning at her as Sir

Walter the Bald repeated the instruction.

'Sword Girl! To the front!'

'Yes, sir!' cried Tommy.

Urging Ned on, she rode to the head of the group. As she lifted her head to gaze at her beloved castle, a flutter of wings above the battlements caught her eye.

'Pigeon!' she called.

There was a flurry of feathers as the pigeon swooped down to fly beside her. 'Sword Girl, you did it – you've saved us!' he crowed.

'No, Pigeon; *we* did it!'

And to the sound of deafening cheers both inside and outside the castle, they led the knights home.

JOIN TOMMY AND
HER FRIENDS FOR ANOTHER
SWORD GIRL
ADVENTURE IN

TOURNAMENT
Trouble

CHAPTER 1

'Flamant for victory!'

The battle cry was so loud it carried through the thick stone walls of the armoury and all the way to the sword chamber where Tommy was working.

'Flamant for victory!'

The cry was echoed by dozens of voices, followed by the thunder of horses' hooves across the great courtyard of Flamant

Castle. The castle's squires were practising their jousting skills in preparation for the tournament that was only five days away.

Tommy held up the sword she was polishing and saw the blade gleam in the flickering light of the candle on the wall. With a sigh, she replaced it in the rack then picked up another sword from the pile on the floor beside her and dipped her rag into the pot of clove-scented oil.

The squires, who were training to be knights, would be jousting with lances on horseback, but the knights themselves would be competing in sword fights. The knights had been practising every day, and Tommy had been polishing and sharpening their swords from morning till night. In all the months she had been

Keeper of the Blades, she had never been so busy.

The cries of the squires were drowned out by a clatter as Reynard, the Keeper of the Bows, burst into the armoury and dropped an armful of shields on the smith's wooden table.

'You've been gone a while,' the smith observed with a grunt. 'Busy in town, is it?'

'You should see it, Smith,' Reynard replied. 'All the houses have banners on them in the colours of Flamant Castle, and the town is full of merchants who've come from all over for the fair in Jonglers Field.'

Tommy, who had lifted her head from her work to listen, ducked it again when she saw Reynard glance in her direction. Reynard had hated Tommy ever since she

had been made the Keeper of the Blades
instead of him.

But Reynard must have seen that
Tommy was listening for he raised his
voice to say, 'There are going to be dancers
and musicians – I even saw some acrobats
practising their tumbling. I feel sorry for
anyone who's missing all the fun.'

Reynard didn't sound very sorry at all, Tommy thought, as she scrubbed furiously at a smudge of dirt on the blade of a sword. She had been so excited when Sir Walter the Bald announced that Flamant Castle would be holding a tournament, and all the knights and squires of neighbouring Roses Castle had been invited. There was to be a grand procession followed by three days of competitions, with a big feast held every night. And on top of that, there was to be a fair in Jonglers Field, with stalls and games and entertainment. Tommy longed to see the preparations, but whenever Smith needed an errand run to the blacksmith in town, he sent Reynard instead of her. 'I'm sorry, Sword Girl,' he would say, 'but you're needed here.'

Tommy sighed again.

'What's the matter, dearie?'

The voice came from a sabre behind her. It was Nursie, one of the Old Wrecks. When Tommy had first become Keeper of the Blades, responsible for looking after all the bladed weapons of Flamant Castle, the Old Wrecks had been neglected for years. But Tommy soon discovered that the swords in the small rack in the darkest corner of the sword chamber were inhabited by the spirits of their previous owners.

'I'm just thinking about the tournament,' Tommy told her.

'Ooh, the tournament,' said Nursie. 'What an exciting time. Why, I remember when my little darling fought in his first tournament. He won, of course.' Nursie's 'little darling', Tommy knew, was Sir Walter himself; Nursie had been his nursemaid.

A long-handled dagger with a deep voice chimed in, 'And don't forget the fair. All those stalls … There'll be leather goods and delicious pies and spices and candles and – oh, anything you can imagine. It's a fine time to be a merchant. Will you be buying anything at the fair, Sword Girl?'

'You merchants are all the same, Bevan Brumm,' Nursie scolded. 'Always wanting people to buy things. But our sword girl is more interested in the tournament, aren't you, dearie?'

While the sabre and the dagger

argued over which was better, a tournament or a fair, Tommy's spirits sank lower. She'd never seen a tournament *or* a fair.

As she sighed for a third time, a slender sword with a slightly curved blade spoke up. 'It must be hard to be cooped up here in the sword chamber when there's so much excitement going on outside.' Jasper Swann, a squire, had been close to Tommy's own age when he died. Perhaps that was why he often seemed to understand what she was feeling.

Tommy looked at the sword in her hand. 'I wish I could be out there in the courtyard,' she said. 'Riding a horse and jousting.' She thrust the sword forward at an imaginary opponent. It was Tommy's dearest wish to one day become a squire. 'But they'll probably never let a girl ride in a tournament,' she finished gloomily.

'Don't be downhearted, dearie,' Nursie advised. 'Your turn will come.'

'That's right, Sword Girl,' Jasper agreed. 'After all, whoever thought a kitchen girl would become the castle's Keeper of the Blades? And look how quickly you—'

But before he could finish they heard a cry so loud it made Tommy drop her sword in fright. 'What was that?' she gasped.

ABOUT THE AUTHOR

FRANCES WATTS was born in the medieval city of Lausanne, in Switzerland, and moved to Australia when she was three. After studying literature at university she began working as an editor. Her bestselling picture books include *Kisses for Daddy* and the 2008 Children's Book Council of Australia award-winner, *Parsley Rabbit's Book about Books* (both illustrated by David Legge). Frances is also the author of a series about two very unlikely superheroes, Extraordinary Ernie and Marvellous Maud, and the highly acclaimed children's fantasy/adventure series, the Gerander Trilogy.

Frances lives in Sydney's inner west, and divides her time between writing and editing. Her cat doesn't talk.

ABOUT THE ILLUSTRATOR

GREGORY ROGERS has always loved art and drawing so it's no surprise he became an illustrator. He was the first Australian to win the prestigious Kate Greenaway Medal. The first of his popular wordless picture book series, *The Boy, the Bear, the Baron, the Bard,* was selected as one of the Ten Best Illustrated Picture Books of 2004 by the *New York Times* and short-listed for the Children's Book Council of Australia Book of the Year Award in 2005. The third book, *The Hero of Little Street,* won the CBCA Picture Book of the Year in 2010. Gregory loves movies and music, and is a collector of books, antiques and anything odd and unusual.

He lives in Brisbane above a bookshop cafe with his cat Sybil.

THE *Terrible* TRICKSTER

'Tricksters are not welcome here.'

A trickster is turning life at Flamant Castle upside down. Someone has put sneezing powder in the knights' soup and itching powder in Sir Walter's sheets and changed the salt for sugar in Mrs Moon's kitchen. At first the tricks seem funny, but Sir Benedict is not amused. He thinks the trickster is Tommy – and unless the tricks stop, he will send her away from the castle! Can she find out who the real trickster is before she is banished forever?

Pigeon PROBLEMS

'The pigeon is missing!'

It's Lady Beatrix's birthday, and Sir Walter is planning a celebration at Flamant Castle. There will be games and competitions and a big surprise party. Everyone at the castle is excited … except the pigeon. But the pigeon is needed for a very special job – and when he goes missing, it looks like Sir Walter's plans will be ruined. Can Tommy find her friend and save the celebrations?